For Lauren Farquharson & Ross Hooper, with love ~ PB

For my little angel, with love from mummy ~ SL

Bloomsbury Publishing, London, New Delhi, New York and Sydney

First published in Great Britain in 2015 by Bloomsbury Publishing Plc
50 Bedford Square, London, WC1B 3DP

A CIP catalogue record for this book is available from the British Library

ISBN 978 1 4088 3969 0 (HB)
ISBN 978 1 4088 3970 6 (PB)
ISBN 978 1 4088 3968 3 (eBook)

Printed in China by Leo Paper Products, Heshan, Guangdong

1 3 5 7 9 10 8 6 4 2

www.bloomsbury.com

BLOOMSBURY is a registered trademark of Bloomsbury Publishing Plc

All papers used by Bloomsbury Publishing are natural, recyclable products
made from wood grown in well-managed forests.
The manufacturing processes conform to the environmental regulations of the country of origin

YIKES, Ticklysaurus!

Pamela Butchart
& Sam Lloyd

BLOOMSBURY

LONDON NEW DELHI NEW YORK SYDNEY

Down by the hot and muddy swamp,
the dinos were all glum.
"I'm bored!" sighed Brontosaurus.
"We really need some fun."

So UP jumped Ticklysaurus
and gave his arms a wiggle.
"Quick, run, it's time for TICKLE CHASE –
I'll make you dinos giggle."

1, 2, 3...

YIKES, Ticklysaurus!

Brontosaurus sprinted off,
and laughed,

"You can't catch me!"

But Ticklysaurus
got to work –

OOPS!

Bronto did a wee!

"Not my horns!" squealed Triceratops.
"Please don't tickle there!"
But tickle, tickle, wiggle, giggle
Ticklysaurus didn't care.

Stegosaurus hid in a cave
but there was something he'd forgotten,
so **tickle, tickle, wiggle, giggle**
Tickly tickled him on the bottom.

Pterodactyl cleverly
flew up into a tree.
But **tickle, tickle, wiggle, giggle**
Tickly's arms reached easily.

The dinosaurs dashed and crashed.
They ran and stomped about.

Diplodocus splashed in the lake –
but soon got tickled out!

"We're exhausted," said the dinos.
"No more TICKLE CHASE today."

But Tickly waved his spaghetti arms.
He STILL wanted to play.

YIKES, Ticklysaurus!

There was just one dino out there
who hadn't yet joined in.
The loudest, scariest of them all
made Tickly lose his grin.

Did Tickly dare to do it?
He looked T. Rex up and down.
Would a little tickle
banish T. Rex's frown?

"I'm not tickling a T. Rex," said Tickly, "that won't do."

But I think it's time to play a game
of TICKLE CHASE with . . .

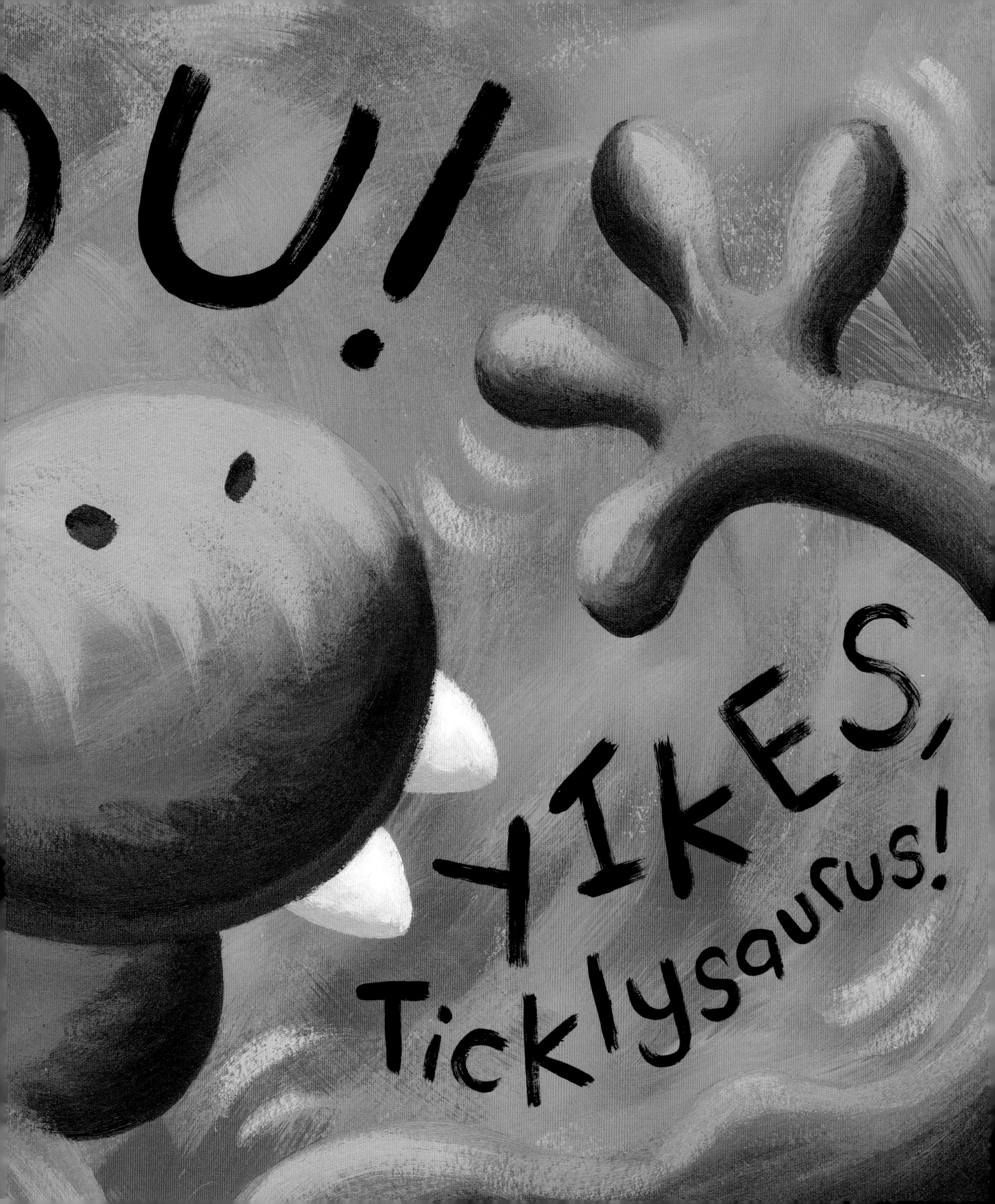

OU!
YIKES,
Ticklysaurus!